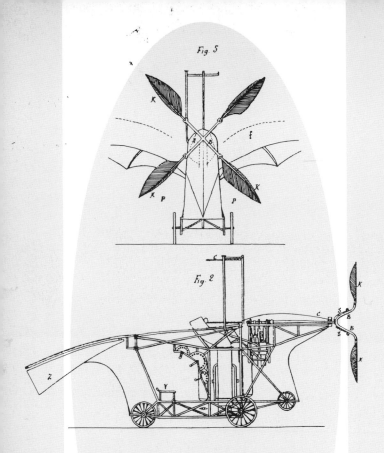

Fig. 5

Fig. 2

Harry N.
Abrams, Inc.
Publishers

Leopold Kapp
lived in a big house
in a little town in southern Bavaria.
His father owned a modest
but thriving biscuit factory,
Kaiserbiscuits.

Leopold's mother had died when he was very young and the boy was often alone. So he climbed trees, ate biscuits, and flew kites. He loved things that fly

In the winter it was bitter cold in the house. Leopold often thought that it must be like living inside an ice cream cone. He had a vivid imagination.

One day, when Leopold was about eighteen, his father called him into his study for a talk. Leopold was concerned because this had rarely happened in his life. He knew he was about to be told something important.

Leopold's father was an old-fashioned businessman, but his biscuit factory survived all the fads that came and went. Other factories made biscuits faster and sweeter and offered a wide variety of new shapes and sizes. But *Kaiserbiscuits* continued to be made as they had been made for nearly one hundred years — in the shapes of animals and boats and dolls.

His father told Leopold that he wanted him to go off to the university at Koenigsdorf to study commerce. The old man pointed to the portraits on the walls of the study and said "Your family has worked in the factory for generations, my boy, and they are observing you. Don't let us down, dear son." ■

And that was the end of their interview. ■

The last thing that Leopold wanted was to go to the university at Koenigsdorf to study commerce, which he did not understand. But he packed his wicker trunk with a top hat, some dozen black ties, one of his father's frock coats, and a few books.

He went off to the train station feeling lonely and abandoned. Only the family's old butler came along to see him off. Not even his favorite dog was permitted in the carriage.

The main square of Koenigsdorf was dazzling to Leopold.

He saw the old town gates, the Fildiniptihopf, and the Gothic cathedral, thought to be beautiful, though it was squat and dark.

What he didn't like most
were the other students, who teased
him for his country dress and his country manners.
Unhappy, he found consolation riding his bicycle
on the weekend. And that was how
he met Gustav and Max.

The two haughty young men that Leopold spied at a distance were unusual fellows. Gustav was the son of a viscount. Fascinated by mechanics, he was studying engineering. His teachers didn't think much of him because he had long hair, but he was an aristocrat so they turned a blind eye. ■

Max was the son of a coffee planter in Java. He was studying history, was extremely scholarly, and loved good food almost as much as going fast. ■

He and Gustav had bought the automobile (for that is what it was called) together, and they raced around the countryside at every opportunity. ■

The poor villagers were not happy with this contraption bolting over the roads belching smoke and running down chickens, but there was little they could do. ■

One November day, while Leopold was in the bathtub reading his mail, he opened a letter informing him that his father had died.

A single tear crossed his cheek. Now he was truly alone in the world.

But he had an inheritance. Leopold spent no time grieving. He began his new life by buying a jaunty cap and installing a gasoline engine on his bicycle. The next Sunday he entered a race for all vehicles and crossed the finish line well ahead of Gustav and Max.

Like the sportsmen they were, Gustav and Max congratulated Leopold. They admired his motor-driven bicycle and he praised their stylish automobile. They discovered that they had much in common.

And there began a great friendship among the three young men. They promised to meet again soon.

One day Gustav and Max invited Leopold for tea. The talk was lively, for they shared many interests, mainly a love of going fast and far. They discussed the relative merits of automobiles versus motorcycles, argued the virtues of steam yachts over sail, and speculated whether someday man might travel beneath the sea. "Impossible," said Gustav, "although I have read of a Spanish major who claims to have done it. It sounds fishy to me."

Then, while Max was pouring another cup of tea, Leopold revealed to his friends something he had never shared with anyone. "I intend to fly," he said, and the three knew at once that this was why they had come together—to find a way of conquering the air.

Excitedly they set up a plan for inventing a flying machine. First, they reasoned, they should explore history to find any precedents, any sign that someone in the past had ventured aloft.

Next day they huddled in the back row of one of Max's lectures on ancient history and heard the professor exclaim about the high cultural achievements of the pharaohs in Egypt. Mummification was only one of many fascinating subjects touched on. Could it be that among these dusty records there was a hint of flying? "Doubtful," whispered Max, "In all the papyri I have studied there isn't one reference to aerial activity. Pyramid building, yes. Flying, no."

Gustav was impatient. "If history doesn't have anything to offer, with all due respect to you, Max, then science surely does. I recommend we immediately go to the engineering department. My professors are certain to have some good advice." And so, after a hearty lunch at the Café Sacher, they hurried off to the laboratories.

Spying some interesting models in a back room, they tip-toed in to have a look around.

The room the boys had found was the abandoned workroom of Professor Heinrich Ganswindt, an eccentric genius who had blown himself up during some experiments with a hydrogen-filled gasbag. There were models of flying machines, notebooks, and a dusty portrait of Ganswindt himself.

Unable to explore further without arousing suspicion, they left, thinking that were many things here they should know more about.

Next day, at a regatta, Leopold urged Gustav and Max to join him in a daring scheme. They must, he argued, remove Ganswindt's journals from the storeroom. The faculty weren't interested in flight, but they were, so it was only fair that they should have the benefit of Ganswindt's research.

Leopold's passion swayed the others, and they shortly began plotting the theft.

Gustav knew that the storeroom of the engineering building opened onto a back garden. Max knew that the fire company had a wheeled ladder—cart that was used for second-story rescues. With stealth the ladder could be moved in the middle of the night and set up beneath the storeroom window. Entry would be easy, only minutes needed to lift the notebooks, and soon they could be on the street again.

In fact the theft was so easy to carry off and so successful that the next night the boys gave themselves a sumptuous dinner at the Café Sacher. To mark the occasion they even had a menu printed. This is what it contained:

Soupe a l'aviateur
Suprêmes de volaille vaporeux
Sorbet aeolian
Steak au poivre Daedalus
Soufflé stratosphérique

Les vins
Moulin au vent
Champagne celestiale

Afterward, in Max's rooms, they toasted the great enterprise, recording their solemn oath to conquer the air on one of Edison's wax cylinder recording machines.

Work began in earnest the next morning. Ganswindt's plans were for a large balloon made of oiled canvas to be filled with a gas lighter than air. The question was which gas to use.

Hydrogen, as Ganswindt had discovered to his lasting regret, was out of the question. Helium was very expensive but had the virtue of being nonflammable. Freon, neon, argon, and methane were proposed and discarded, the latter because in addition to being highly volatile, its odor was something less than desirable.

Max did prodigious research in the library and it was finally agreed that helium was the only sensible answer. Leopold pledged part of his inheritance to buy it.

How to move the gas bag through the air and how to carry passengers and crew were the next questions.

After lengthy discussion it was decided that since air was, after all, a liquid, the tried-and-true solution was a boat. The vessel's hull would provide a container for the aviators. And as for power, oars and sails would provide forward motion as they did on a boat. No sooner said than done, the trio had rigged up their first flying machine.

Leopold and his friends set sail the next morning from the lawn of the university and made their way slowly over the narrow streets of the town, flying low so they could chat with passersby and calm them. Their strategy had just the opposite effect; horses bolted, dogs barked, and the Rector of the university scowled.

Discretion being called for, they quickly discarded ballast and, just as Ganswindt's calculations had predicted, rose into the air.

The airship rose and rose.
And it rose still more. The crew
began to feel dizzy. The town
below looked like a toy. In the distance
they saw rivers flowing together and the great
Rhine with a naval corvette on maneuvers.

But by then they had lost control
and were drifting west at the
mercy of the wind

Flugapparate

The oars proved useless, the sails only served to make them slaves to the strong breezes, and the tiny propeller that Leopold had devised did little more than fan their faces. Before they knew it night came, and they fell asleep.

They woke stuck to the top of a huge steel tower. In the air nearby, a variety of lighter-than-air machines cavorted, as if flying was the easiest thing in the world.

For this was Paris, where Montgolfier had triumphed and the hot air balloon was nearly as common as the bicycle as a mode of transport and delight.

What a city, the three friends marveled!

Le précurseur

Paris before the turn of the century offered a panoply of myriad pleasures. Climbing down from the marvelous tower, the aeronauts drank it all in, and more besides.

The most fragrant smells filled the air; cafés gave off seductive scents of exotic aperitifs and subtle eaux des vies; boulangeries emitted delicious clouds bearing the aromas of fresh croissants and apricot tarts.

And the ladies, oh the ladies, did they not float through the streets like flower gardens in high bloom? Narrow-waisted, elegantly coiffed, walking their equally well-groomed canine pets, the ladies were a joy to see.

Amusements of all kinds attracted the eye; gaming halls and billiard parlors, and museums of wax figures, and cosmoramas, and most intriguing of all, the kinetoscope.

For a franc each, they entered a darkened salon where the most delectable pleasures were projected on a wall. There, everyone could spin out their fantasies.

Alas, the many charms of Paris were costly and almost before the three friends knew it they had run out of money. Not knowing how far they might travel on their maiden voyage they had come away from Koenigsdorf with barely enough for a brief local journey. Moreover, they had brought neither fresh clothing nor toilet kits.

Now, they were forced to make their way back home on foot.

Elated by their experiences, they were nevertheless exhausted, and badly in need of the services of a barber and a tailor.

What is worse, they were still not convinced that they had learned any secrets of flight when they at last arrived back at the university.

The Rector was furious. He was on the point of expelling each one of them when Gustav's father intervened. Instead of being disciplined, and because they had arrived just at the end of the semester, they were allowed to go off to the seashore for a holiday.

There, they determined, they would find a new solution to the question of flight.

Clearly, a balloon was not the answer. Difficult to control in its elevation and almost completely at the mercy of the prevailing winds, a balloon would never satisfy their wish for fully independent flight. They needed to come up with a device that could make its way through the sky as freely as a bird.

Back at school Gustav continued his diligent routine of exercise. He spent long hours in the gym lifting weights, and doing tumbling routines. His purpose in all this was a mystery to his friends.

Max, meanwhile, made a specialty of gourmet eating, while Leopold studied the flight of gulls.

Finally the reason for Gustav's fanatical fitness training was discovered.

Inspired by Leonardo da Vinci's sketches, he had built an ornithopter made of bamboo cane and cloth. Max and Leopold had known nothing about it.

Next Friday Gustav invited his friends to his father's country estate. A large crowd of guests gathered on Saturday morning. They watched Gustav climb to the roof of the main house. After a moment's pause he precipitously launched himself into the air. Athlete though he was, no manner of flapping could keep him aloft. After gliding some yards he crashed in a tumble.

Unhurt but humiliated, Gustav rode back to Koenigsdorf with the others. They were no closer to the secret of flight.

The next night, tossing and turning in his bed, Leopold wrestled with their dilemma. He realized that Gustav was on to something by experimenting with the bird wing. He knew from years of having watched birds in flight that the form was perfect.

The problem was that with all of Gustav's physical training, he was not strong enough. There was no way he could pull his weight through the air fast enough to to defy gravity with his manmade bird wing. A sparrow, in relation to its size, had far stronger pectoral muscles than Gustav. Power, Leopold reasoned, was the answer. Power coupled with the mysterious geometry of the bird's wing that produces the indispensable "lift."

Leopold shrieked with joy and ran downstairs to tell the others.

That summer Gustav rented a large country property with vast open fields so they could pursue their experiments.

The three friends devised a variety of models with birdlike wings and a propeller driven by twisted rubber bands.

They learned much about aerodynamics, but realized that to make anything larger than a small model would require more than rubber bands.

Still without a clear idea of what to use for a power source but impatient to proceed, the three friends built a prototype flying machine which they called *Drachenvogel*.

Gustav designed a pair of large, elegant birdlike wings for its main supports. Max drew upon all his classical avian references in decorating the machine, and Leopold wondered how on earth this giant beast would ever ascend. Well, of course, without an engine of any kind, it never did. It weighed at least as much as a school bus and was about as airworthy as a bathtub. In fact, pointed headfirst into a gale force wind, *Drachenvogel* didn't even shudder.

For their second model, the aeronauts trimmed the fuselage, or body, of the aircraft to some semblance of ornithological proportion.

They installed within it a steam-driven rotary engine that turned a crankshaft linked to a parasol-like propeller. Feather-covered wings and an ornate tail completed the ensemble. With a parrot-like beak and a pair of portholes for navigation, the creation at least resembled a bird in its general appearance.

As a final aid in achieving an airborne state, the inventors devised a catapult launching platform. When Leopold strapped himself into the pilot's seat he was confident that he soon would soar. ∎

But *Le Perroquet* only made it to the end of the catapult ramp before tumbling beak over bottom into a pile of twisted bamboo and singed feathers.

Gustav's cousin, Princess Thyra, came to visit during the building of the third model. Poor Gustav was so smitten by her that he was very little help. The others worked on, creating a lighter and more birdlike aircraft, powered by Leopold's motorcycle engine and dubbed Junggans.

On his first trial, with Leopold again as pilot, the creature shook, staggered, and hopped its way along the ground in three great bounds, finally managing to become airborne for about twenty feet before diving into a flower bed. The inventors were jubilant. Thyra, looking on, was bored.

Leopold was now convinced that with more power and a better weight-to-power ratio they could achieve sustained flight. ►

"If only we could have your engine, Gustav. It is much more powerful than mine. We could fly, I'm sure," pleaded Leopold.

"The engine of my automobile? That's impossible," said Gustav, "I need my car for outings with Thyra," and so ended the discussion. ■

At this point, Gustav abandoned them altogether. Too busy courting cousin Thyra, he was no longer compelled by the quest that had driven them on. But there was more bad news in store for Leopold and Max. University officials had been petitioned by the town council to put an end to the noisy and dangerous experiments. Complaints had been lodged, summonses were in process, fines were levied. In brief and in sum, Leopold and Max were expelled from the university.

With the remnant of his inheritance, Leopold rented a house near the sea where he and Max could continue their experiments. Max was disheartened.

"Why do we need to fly" he said. "Life on earth is complicated enough."

"Don't you see," argued Leopold, "man has already mastered travel on land with trains and motorcars, and at sea with steamships. Why should we be inferior to birds? Even the lowly mosquito has the advantage of us. Besides, we have already proved, after centuries of being stuck to the earth like snails, that man can fly."

"But only eight inches off the ground," moaned Max.

"Yes, but that was because we had too small an engine. A lighter airframe and more horsepower will do the trick. We're on the brink, I feel sure."

"The only thing we're on the brink of," Max sighed, "is the cliff we're sitting on." But he agreed to carry on. ▚

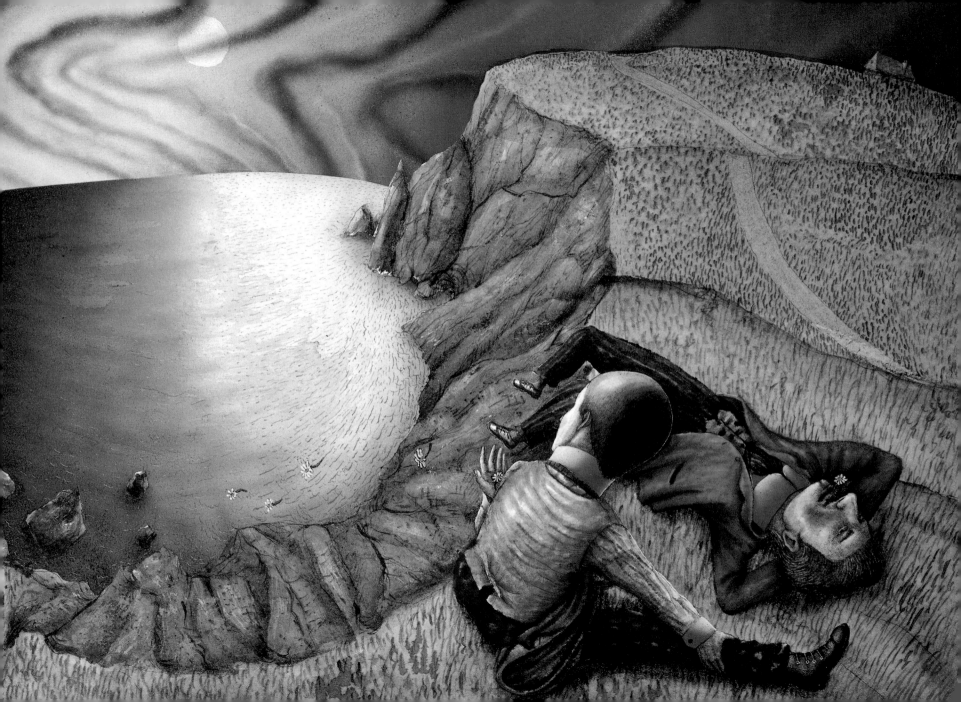

In the barn of their rented house Leopold and Max set out to build another engine and fashion another craft to conquer the air. Within a few days of beginning, however, a deputation of local citizens banged on their door.

"Open up in the name of the law!," a stern voice demanded.

The burgomeister, the priest, and several notable townsfolk were there to inspect the laboratory. Two strong forest rangers had come along to make sure that order was kept. Rumor had it, stated the burgomeister, that secret experiments were being conducted in the barn, and that dangerous explosives were in use.

"Nothing could be further from the truth," explained Leopold. He then proceeded to tell the townspeople about his dream and the long history of their failed attempts. The country-dwellers were little swayed by Leopold's argument that man needed to fly. They saw little use even in the railroad that crossed their country. But since it appeared that the only damage this mad pair could do would be to themselves, the inventors were left to continue in peace. The children of the town, however, perennially curious, were forbidden to go near the place. ■

Over the next weeks, as Leopold and Max labored on a delicately-framed vehicle dubbed Uhu, they were visited by a shy boy on crutches. Leopold tried to warn him away, remembering the burgomeister's injunctions, but he seemed determined.

"I'm fourteen, and no child," the boy said. He was Oskar, son of the local blacksmith, who had lost his right foot when a stallion stepped on him. The cheerful lad had a real mechanical gift and before long he was wielding a wrench here and a ratchet there.

When the new airplane was finally ready, Max painted an owl's face on its nose, hoping that the emblem of this master flier of the night would serve them well.

Leopold put the final touches on a sturdy three-cylinder engine that was hooked up to drive not one but two propellers. Maintaining the tautness of the propeller belts was something of a problem and controlling the fuel flow to the cylinders was difficult, but Leopold believed that all would come right on the day of the test. Oskar was full of excitement.

Gustav and Thyra were notified and promised to drive over to witness the launching.

What they saw the next day was a disaster. Uhu's engine exploded and Leopold crashed in a pile of flames not twenty feet from where he had begun. A farmer's haystack went up in smoke with the craft.

Leopold was far from alone, however, for Oskar, the blacksmith's son, had become his faithful aide and helper. Oskar came to believe as fervently as Leopold that they could conquer the air, and he was a quick student of the mechanics of airframe building. With his small, strong hands he became adept at tying together the intricate web of bamboo struts that formed the wings of Number 5, dubbed *Schwalbe*, or swift, by Leopold.

With the last remnant of his inheritance, Leopold bought a brand new model

of gasoline engine, far more powerful and reportedly more reliable than any he had used before.

Month after month, he and Oskar worked over the Schwalbe, refining the angle of the wings, adjusting their curvature, and carving an elegant wooden propeller for the nose cone.

They stretched and painted the fabric skin of the fuselage so that there wasn't a wrinkle on it. By November 15, 1903, they had finished their work.

"When are you going to fly it?" asked Oskar, "I can't wait to go."

"I'm afraid I can't permit that, Oskar, it's far too dangerous. We've had nothing but crashes. I don't even know when I will go. I am filled with doubt," said Leopold.

That night Leopold restlessly paced the floor of the workshop, turning over in his mind all the failed attempts, all the vain hopes, all the new calculations. Finally, just before a rosy dawn peeped through the low-hanging clouds, he made his resolve.

He wheeled Schwalbe into the meadow beside the shop and pointed her nose toward the sea.

"It's better that Oskar doesn't see me if I go down," he thought. "The poor boy would be heartbroken."

And with that, he made a final check-up walk around the airplane, as pilots would do for generations thereafter. Satisfied, he leaned into the cockpit to set the controls and returned forward. As if he had done it a thousand times before, he cranked the propeller. The engine caught. Leopold climbed aboard, settled himself, advanced the throttle, and took off. Just as he had dreamed, he was flying.

The next morning Oskar arrived to find the workshop empty. He searched in vain over the meadow.

He walked along the moor, and to the edge of the cliff. The beach below was empty, and the sea showed its implacable face.

Oskar spent the whole day gazing at the sky and wondering what had become of Leopold. He was not sad, but lonely.

Each day of the passing years, Oskar remembered the last time he had seen Leopold. It was exactly one month before news came from America that the Wright brothers had made the world's first successful flight.

Oskar knew differently. And sometimes when he walked beside the sea, he was certain that he could see a large winged creature wheeling above the cliffs — a swift with a smile on its face.

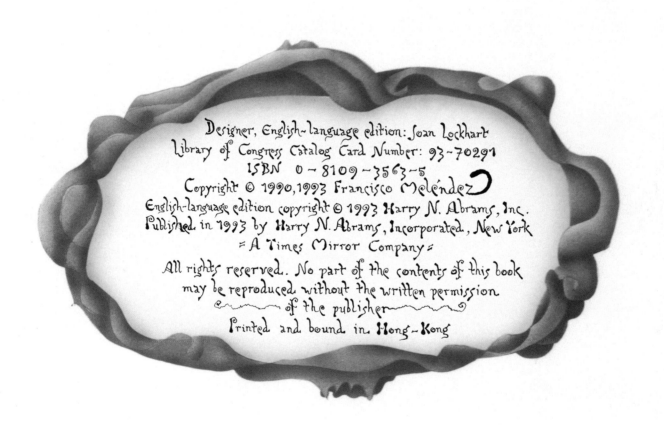

Designer, English~language edition: Joan Lockhart
Library of Congress Catalog Card Number: 93~70291
ISBN 0 ~ 8109 ~ 3563 ~ 5
Copyright © 1990,1993 Francisco Meléndez
English~language edition copyright © 1993 Harry N. Abrams, Inc.
Published in 1993 by Harry N. Abrams, Incorporated, New York
= A Times Mirror Company =

Printed and bound in Hong~Kong

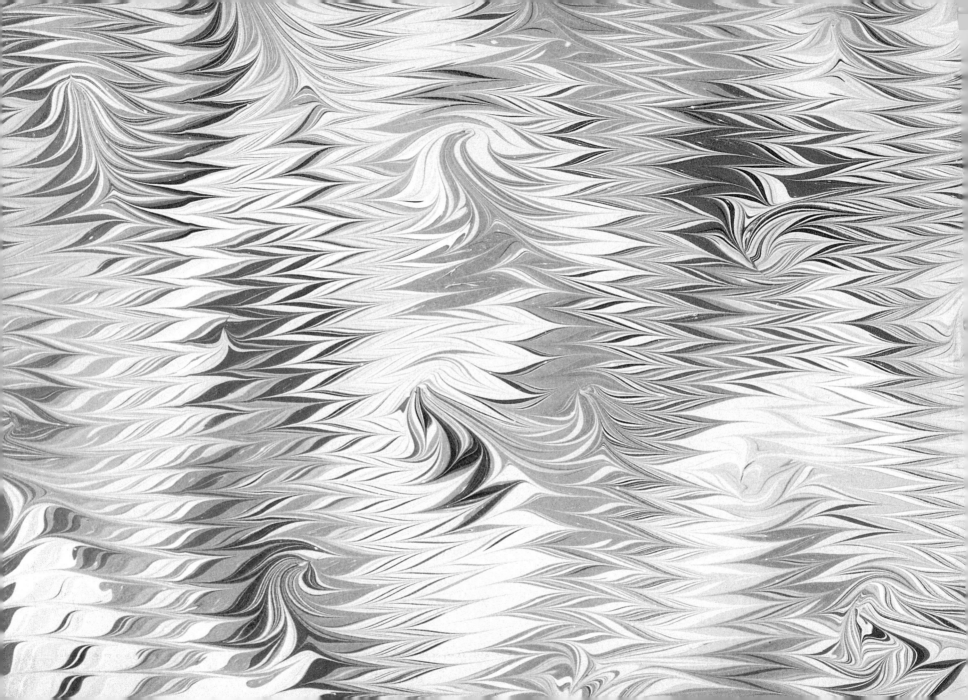